WORLD OF DINOSAURS

THEY LIVED WITH THE DINOSAURS

For a free color catalog describing Gareth Stevens' list of high-quality books and multimedia programs, call 1-800-542-2595 (USA) or 1-800-461-9120 (Canada). Gareth Stevens Publishing's Fax: (414) 225-0377.

Library of Congress Cataloging-in-Publication Data

Fisher, Enid.
    They lived with the dinosaurs/by Enid Fisher; illustrated by Richard Grant.
       p. cm. — (World of dinosaurs)
    Includes bibliographical references and index.
    Summary: Describes the various smaller prehistoric creatures that lived alongside the dinosaurs, including early crocodilians, shrewlike mammals, spiders, dragonflies, primitive frogs, and flying reptiles.
    ISBN 0-8368-2292-7 (lib. bdg.)
    1. Fossils—Juvenile literature. [1. Prehistoric animals.]
I. Grant, Richard, 1959- ill. II. Title. III. Series: World of dinosaurs.
QE714.5.F57   1999
560—dc21   98-45742

This North American edition first published in 1999 by
Gareth Stevens Publishing
1555 North RiverCenter Drive, Suite 201
Milwaukee, Wisconsin 53212 USA

This U.S. edition © 1999 by Gareth Stevens, Inc.
Created with original © 1998 by Quartz Editorial Services, 112 Station Road, Edgware HA8 7AQ U.K.
Additional end matter © 1999 by Gareth Stevens, Inc.

Consultant: Dr. Paul Barrett, Paleontologist, Specialist in Biology and Evolution of Dinosaurs, University of Cambridge, England.

All rights reserved. No part of this book may be reproduced, stored in a retrieval system, or transmitted in any form or by any means, electronic, mechanical, photocopying, or otherwise without the prior written permission of the copyright holder.

Printed in Mexico

1 2 3 4 5 6 7 8 9 03 02 01 00 99

WORLD OF DINOSAURS

THEY LIVED WITH THE DINOSAURS

by Enid Fisher
Illustrated by Richard Grant

Gareth Stevens Publishing
MILWAUKEE

CONTENTS

Introduction.............................5

On the seabed..........................6

Teeming swamp life 8

Prehistoric creepy-crawlies............10

Flowering landscapes..................12

Flying reptiles........................14

Mammal gallery........................16

Coastal gallery.......................18

Gallery of plants.....................20

Living fossils........................22

In the salty seas.....................24

Winged lizards........................26

Ready for take-off....................28

For more information..................30

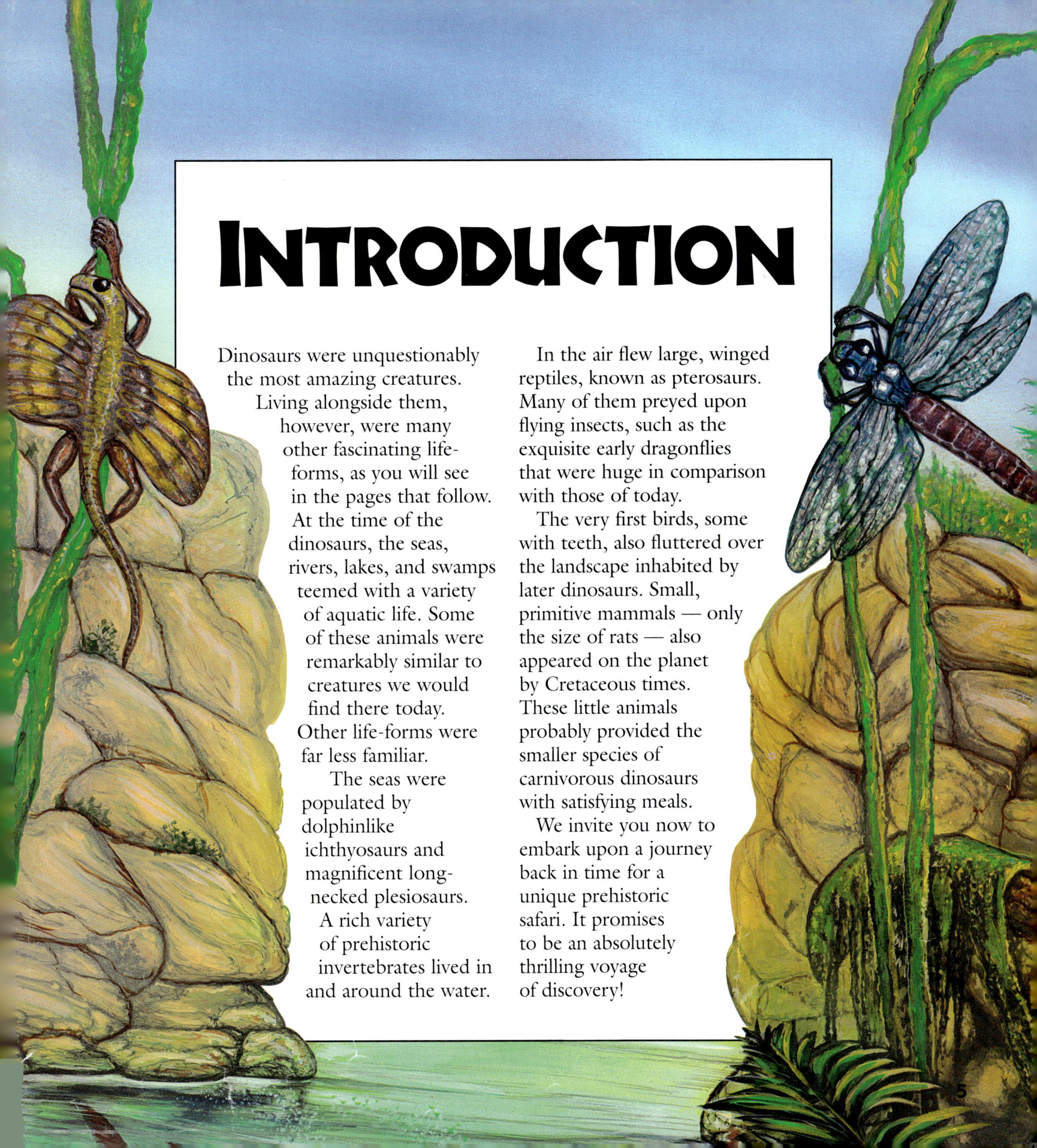

INTRODUCTION

Dinosaurs were unquestionably the most amazing creatures. Living alongside them, however, were many other fascinating life-forms, as you will see in the pages that follow. At the time of the dinosaurs, the seas, rivers, lakes, and swamps teemed with a variety of aquatic life. Some of these animals were remarkably similar to creatures we would find there today. Other life-forms were far less familiar.

The seas were populated by dolphinlike ichthyosaurs and magnificent long-necked plesiosaurs. A rich variety of prehistoric invertebrates lived in and around the water.

In the air flew large, winged reptiles, known as pterosaurs. Many of them preyed upon flying insects, such as the exquisite early dragonflies that were huge in comparison with those of today.

The very first birds, some with teeth, also fluttered over the landscape inhabited by later dinosaurs. Small, primitive mammals — only the size of rats — also appeared on the planet by Cretaceous times. These little animals probably provided the smaller species of carnivorous dinosaurs with satisfying meals.

We invite you now to embark upon a journey back in time for a unique prehistoric safari. It promises to be an absolutely thrilling voyage of discovery!

ON THE SEABED

Although dinosaurs did not inhabit the prehistoric seas, these vast stretches of water were by no means empty. In fact, they teemed with all sorts of life, as you can see in this illustration. These aquatic creatures must have seemed strange to the dinosaurs that ventured to the water's edge to quench their thirst!

The sauropod bent its seemingly endless neck toward the water. It was preparing to quench a thirst worked up by a frantic run from a marauding predator. The Jurassic sea was cool and clear; as the massive sauropod lowered its head closer to the surface, it suddenly became aware of a mass of small creatures moving around in the water and on the seabed.

Many tiny sea-dwellers lived during the 160 million years that the dinosaurs ruled planet Earth. Among the most common were the ammonites, squidlike mollusks that lived in their own coiled shells. Some grew up to 6.5 feet (2 meters) in diameter, although most were only a few inches (cm) across. They lived alongside their cousins, the belemnites, which were also somewhat squidlike. The belemnites had an internal skeleton and were similar to modern cuttlefish. Both ammonites and belemnites were once so numerous that thousands of fossils have been found in prehistoric coastal regions. They became extinct by the end of Cretaceous times.

Coral reefs

Many of today's shellfish can boast ancestors that lived alongside the dinosaurs. The Early Triassic seas had been thinly populated, following a mass extinction of sea life about 220 million years ago. By Jurassic times, however, oysters, mussels, shrimp, crabs, and lobsters were well established and abundant. The later Cretaceous seas also contained vast colonies of coral — thousands of living organisms clustered together to form weird shapes in wonderful colors.

Jellyfish, too, abounded during this time, repelling their many predators with the venomous sting for which they are still feared today.

Many species of fish swam in prehistoric waters, even before Triassic times. Some, like **Cornuboniscus**, were very unfishlike in appearance. Called chondrosteans, they had bony armor-plating, especially around the head, and oversized tail fins to keep them buoyant. Only a few descendants of the chondrosteans, such as the sturgeon and the Mississippi paddlefish, survive.

Gradually, fish lost their armor and unwieldy tails, becoming more streamlined like fish of today. Some species, such as Jurassic **Caturus**, were still covered in thick scales, however. A strange survivor, the garpike, found only in some rivers in North America, has scales so robust that spearing weapons bounce off its body.

Fish evolved on a grander scale during Cretaceous times. The fossilized remains of **Xiphacinus**, found in Kansas, for instance, measure 16 feet (5 m) in length. They sported thinner scales, symmetrical bodies, and "ray-fins" — so called because these were supported by long bones or rays. These fish soon overtook their more cumbersome cousins.

TEEMING SWAMP LIFE

Throughout the changing climates of the Triassic, Jurassic, and Cretaceous eras, certain pockets of land were constantly covered with water. These swamps provided a lush habitat for hundreds of semi-aquatic creatures, many of which still exist today.

Warm sunlight dappled the murky waters of the Early Cretaceous swamp. The shadows made it even harder for the wandering **Ouranosaurus** to watch for lurking enemies as it selected a tasty horsetail on which to munch. The crocodilelike **Sarchosuchus**, half-hidden in the reeds that choked the sluggish river, had no such problem. Few creatures passing this massive, 40-ft (12-m)-long creature escaped its snapping jaws — even majestic, sail-backed **Ouranosaurus**. Meandering turtles, with their hard protective shells, kept their distance, too. They feared being flipped over by **Sarchosuchus** and having their soft underbellies exposed to its scythelike teeth.

Swamplands flourished in prehistoric times. They usually resulted from waterlogged river deltas, such as those that fanned out over parts of North Africa and England. The swamps were gloomy places, with forests of high cypresses, gingkoes, and seed-ferns blotting out the light. However, horsetails, mosses, lichens, and the first flowering plants of Cretaceous times grew along the water's edge.

The rulers of the prehistoric swamp-dwellers were ancestors of today's crocodiles, such as the heavily armored **Rutiodon**, which preyed on fish and reptiles. By Cretaceous times, crocodilelike reptiles, such as **Gonipholis**, had evolved into creatures closely resembling the crocodiles found in today's swamps. At 6-10 feet (1.8-3.0 m) in length, they had long, stocky jaws, scaly backs, and clawed feet. These reptilians were ferocious predators.

Turtles, too, have changed little in the 200 million years since they first paddled up and down warm prehistoric river deltas. One of the first, **Proganochelys**, would slither lazily from its muddy perch into the steamy Triassic waters. There, it would trawl the seabed for fish, snails, and clams.

Soft-shelled **Trionyx**, meanwhile, would haul its bulky frame through lush vegetation in pursuit of river prey, such as water scorpions.

Sharing the swamps were a variety of reptiles and amphibians, including the magnificent **Metoposaurus**, a salamanderlike amphibian that grew to over 6 feet (1.8 m) in length. Frogs also populated the reed-beds, darting unobtrusively among the thick vegetation as they flicked their long, sticky tongues to catch passing insects, such as dragonflies.

PREHISTORIC CREEPY-CRAWLIES

Insects were already buzzing in the skies when dinosaurs appeared at the dawn of Triassic times, some 220 million years ago. Smaller carnivorous dinosaurs looked to these insects for a ready supply of food.

Coelophysis had already devoured dozens of the insects that were swarming around the rotting vegetation at the edge of a cool Triassic lake. Still, the large dragonfly that danced before the hungry creature's eyes promised a real feast. The annoying insect had darted away from **Coelophysis**'s snapping jaws just in the nick of time, but its brightly colored body would be its downfall. Glinting in the pale sunlight, it was clearly visible to its predator. Soon, it would sweep past **Coelophysis**'s teeth once too often and then, in one gulp, would be gone.

Scientists believe dragonflies and their graceful look-alikes, the lacewings, have been flying around planet Earth for at least 320 million years. They provided company for large numbers of beetles that were in existence for 400 million years. In fact, many species of creepy-crawlies alive today — including cockroaches, spiders, and grasshoppers — were already very much at home on Earth when the dinosaurs first appeared. Early reptiles probably flourished on a diet of insects and other invertebrates. Some of these tiny creatures even lived as parasites on the dinosaurs, sucking their blood for food.

Many prehistoric invertebrates lived in and around water, feeding on vegetation that rotted in the shallow water or on the moist forest floor. Armies of centipedes and millipedes munched their way through thick carpets of leaf debris, while early mites fed on their droppings. Primitive spiders, such as **Ricinulei**, meanwhile, lurked under fallen logs, waiting quietly to pounce on these unsuspecting browsers.

Certain spider species lived in trees, spinning intricate webs to trap insects feeding on sap that oozed from the bark of conifers. Some insects had an even stickier death. As they were busy eating, they let the sap flow over and trap them. The resin, or sap, hardened, thus preserving the insects in amber tombs for millions of years. In the fictional movie *Jurassic Park*, a prehistoric insect fossilized in amber enables scientists to recreate dinosaurs. The insect had bitten a dinosaur and, in sucking its blood, had taken in some of the ancient reptile's genetic material.

Some prehistoric creepy-crawlies grew to monstrous sizes, much larger than their descendants today. Fossilized dragonflies and grasshoppers with wingspans up to 6 inches (15 cm) have been unearthed. A scorpion that once prowled the prehistoric forests measured an astounding 18 inches (45 cm) from snout to tail.

Invertebrates were not alone on the forest floor. Snakes, too, slithered through the prehistoric landscape, just as they do in regions of the world today. Some may have been poisonous; others may not have been.

FLOWERING LANDSCAPES

Plants in early prehistoric times depended largely on the wind to disperse their seeds and to keep the species going. When flowering plants began to spring up in Early Cretaceous times, however, they secured their survival by encouraging insects to do the job more efficiently through pollination.

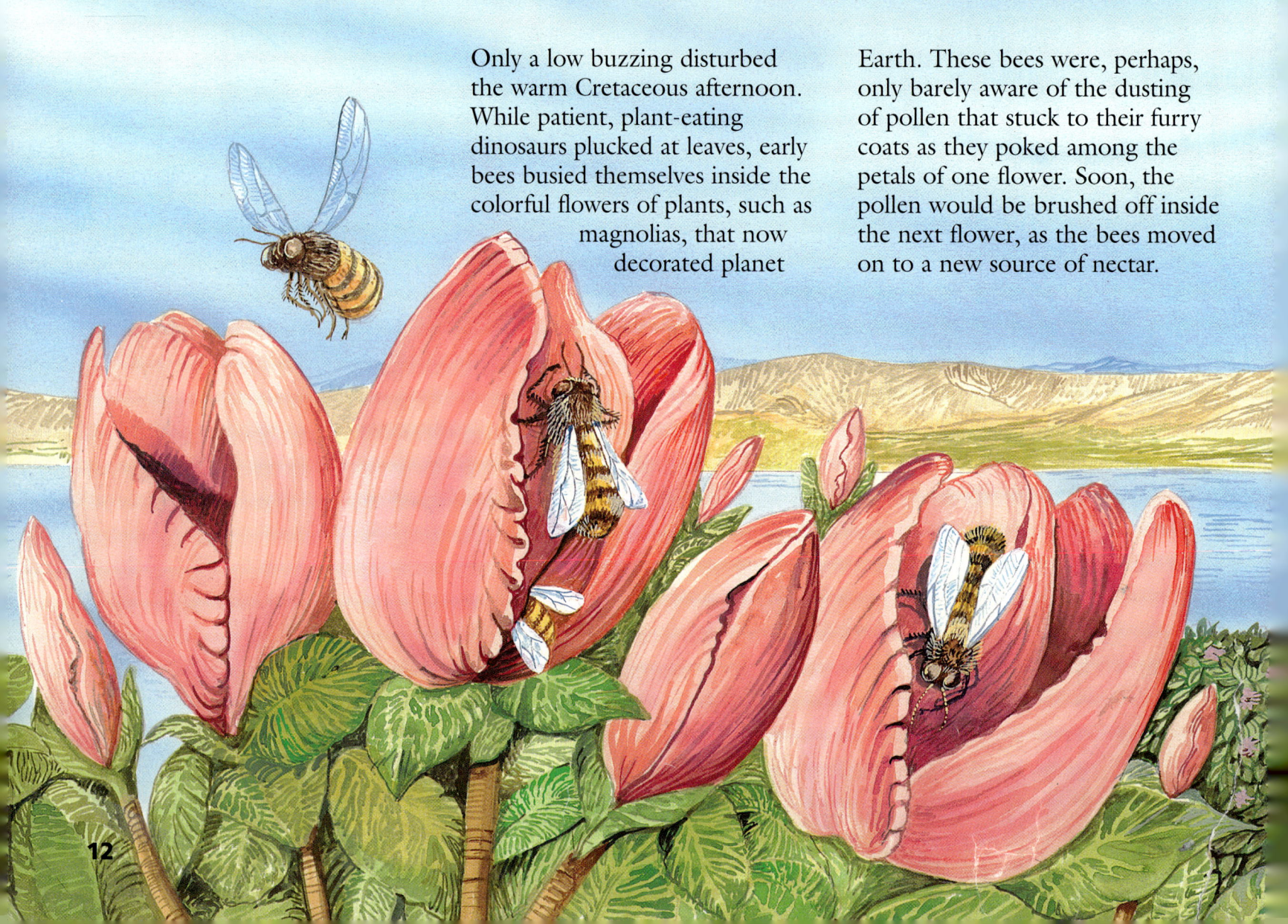

Only a low buzzing disturbed the warm Cretaceous afternoon. While patient, plant-eating dinosaurs plucked at leaves, early bees busied themselves inside the colorful flowers of plants, such as magnolias, that now decorated planet Earth. These bees were, perhaps, only barely aware of the dusting of pollen that stuck to their furry coats as they poked among the petals of one flower. Soon, the pollen would be brushed off inside the next flower, as the bees moved on to a new source of nectar.

These new flowering plants lured insects with the promise of sweet food by means of attractive colors and scents. As the insects traveled from one plant to another, they spread the vital pollen. Before this, seeds had been spread by the wind or scattered when herbivorous dinosaurs excreted what they had eaten in their droppings, known as coprolites when fossilized.

Bees, wasps, butterflies, and moths all became more plentiful and gradually developed a long tongue, called a proboscis, to delve into the depths of the flowers. But, by far, the most successful species to arise in Late Cretaceous times were the true bees. They were equipped with legs that had basketlike receptacles for carrying pollen, like their modern counterparts. These bees also lived in colonies, like bees today, and worked tirelessly to collect nectar and pollen.

Other social insects, such as wasps, ants, and termites, also helped pollinate plants as they explored their prehistoric world in search of food. Scientists believe that one of the earliest flowering plants was the species of magnolia that is still found today in the southern United States. Varieties of roses, waterlilies, laurel, and dogwood also brought color to prehistoric plains and lakes. Many trees — including some specimens that towered up to 300 feet (91 m) over the landscape — produced flowers to attract a variety of high-flying insects.

This was, and still is, a glorious example of symbiosis, in which plants benefit from pollination, and the insects benefit from food. Plant-eating Cretaceous dinosaurs were quick to feast off these new flowering species. New types of dinosaurs also evolved, such as **Parasaurolophus**, shown here. This herbivore had a toothless beak and cheek teeth that were more suited to plucking and chewing soft vegetation than to grinding and crushing the tough cones and fern fronds of earlier types of plants.

FLYING REPTILES

From the earliest age of the dinosaurs, it was clear that, for some species, the environment offered too little food and too many enemies. Nature, however, gave them a way out; they evolved wings and began to fly.

Pteranodon stared at its mate as the two swooped over the clifftops, trying to find a good spot for a nest. Suddenly, a herd of sauropods came into view, far below. These long-necked dinosaurs were herbivores and would probably not attack, so any nest and eggs would most likely be safe. The pteranodons glided down and landed effortlessly. When their young hatched, these parents would be able to scour the sea nearby for fish, bringing them back to their newborn in pelicanlike beaks.

It is possible that the combined quest for safety and a more plentiful food supply drove some prehistoric reptiles into the air. Some experts think that fugitives, fleeing from a pursuing predator, may even have run so fast that they became airborne. Others, however, claim that flying reptiles evolved from winged lizards, which had already mastered the art of gliding by unfurling large membranes attached to the rib bones protruding from their sides. Fossil evidence supports this claim. In fact, alongside the remains of a Triassic winged lizard known as **Longisquama**, found in 1970 in Kirgizstan, Central Asia, were the imprints of a skeleton — named **Podopteryx**, meaning "foot-wing." Its wing membranes were attached, not to elongated ribs, but to its limbs, like those of the first flying reptiles, the pterosaurs.

Pterosaurs had two large forelimbs, each with a thick fourth finger extending outward. Between these forelimbs and their flanks stretched two wafer-thin expanses of skin, which the pterosaur could flap to achieve powered flight.

Some types of flying reptiles were very odd-looking. Chunky **Dimorphodon**, for example, had a short tail and a head shaped like a puffin's. Its mouth was filled with hard, biting teeth that it probably used for devouring flying insects, such as dragonflies. **Rhamphorhynchus**, meanwhile, had a very long tail that ended in a kitelike rudder. Its long beak was filled with vicious, forward-pointing teeth — ideal for spearing fish as the creature swooped low over the ocean.

The most successful species was probably **Pterodactylus**, which flourished from Late Jurassic times. This master of flight was short-tailed and long-beaked, and it lived on fish. Smaller types were pigeon-sized, with a wingspan of 14 inches (35.5 cm), while later cousins boasted an impressive 8-foot (2.4-m) wingspan, about the same as a modern eagle.

These airborne reptiles posed no threat to the dinosaurs. In fact, they may have helped plant-eating types avoid predators. Their screeching and howling probably kept the herbivores alert and provided clear warnings at critical times.

15

MAMMAL

Tritylodont
A 3.5-foot (1-m)-long plant-eater, the Triassic therapsid **Tritylodont** (TRITT-EEL-OH-DONT) was a mammal-like reptile with unusual teeth and a name meaning "three-knobbed tooth." At the back of its jaws, each upper tooth had three strange knobs; each lower tooth had two knobs. There were large fangs at the front of its mouth. Its remains have been found in North America, China, and England.

Triconodon
A mammal from Late Jurassic times, **Triconodon** (TRY-KON-OH-DON) was only about the size of a domestic cat today. Nevertheless, it probably hunted small creatures on which it fed, as you can see here. Remains have been dug up in Europe. It is possible that these predators could climb trees.

GALLERY

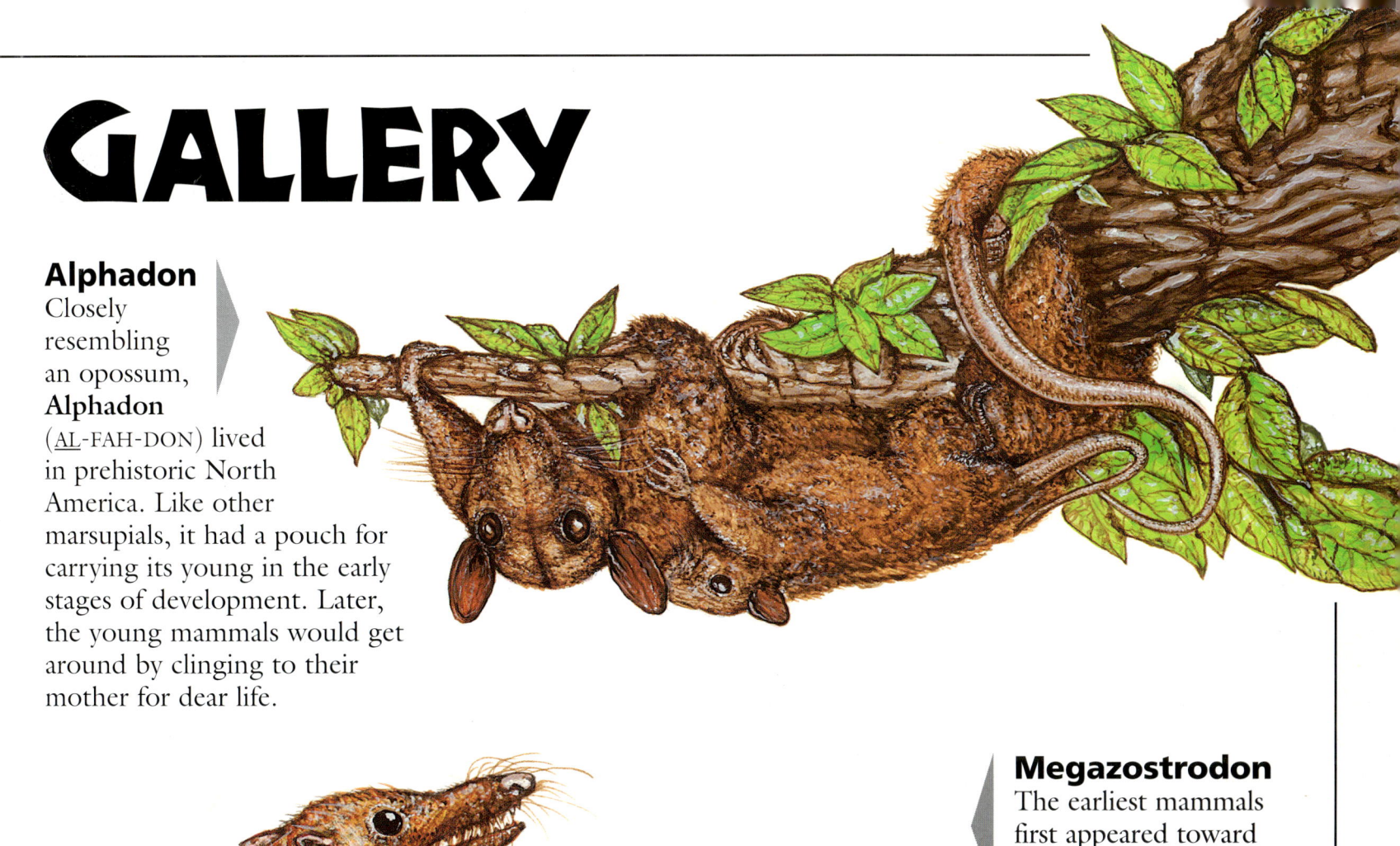

Alphadon
Closely resembling an opossum, **Alphadon** (AL-FAH-DON) lived in prehistoric North America. Like other marsupials, it had a pouch for carrying its young in the early stages of development. Later, the young mammals would get around by clinging to their mother for dear life.

Megazostrodon
The earliest mammals first appeared toward the end of Triassic times. The shrewlike **Megazostrodon** (MEG-AH-ZOS-TROH-DON) was one of them. Tiny and carnivorous, it grew to about 5 inches (13 cm) in length, a bit smaller than the illustration shown here.

17

COASTAL

Labyrinthodont
Unearthed on Australia's southeast coast, **Labyrinthodont** (LAB-ERR-INTH-OH-DONT) was a primitive swimming creature. Recent discoveries reveal, however, that some survived until Cretaceous times. This early amphibian grew to 10 feet (3 m) in length.

Saurosuchus
A carnivorous, crocodilelike reptile from Triassic times, **Saurosuchus** (SAHR-OH-SOOK-US) was about 19 feet (5.8 m) long. It did not live in water but on land, near the coast, much of the time. Remains of this rauisuchian have been found in Argentina.

Rutiodon
Living mainly on fish and small reptiles, **Rutiodon** (ROOT-EE-OH-DON) was a typical phytosaur with large, toothed jaws. It grew to about 16 feet (5 cm) in length. Fossils have been unearthed in Europe, as well as North America.

GALLERY

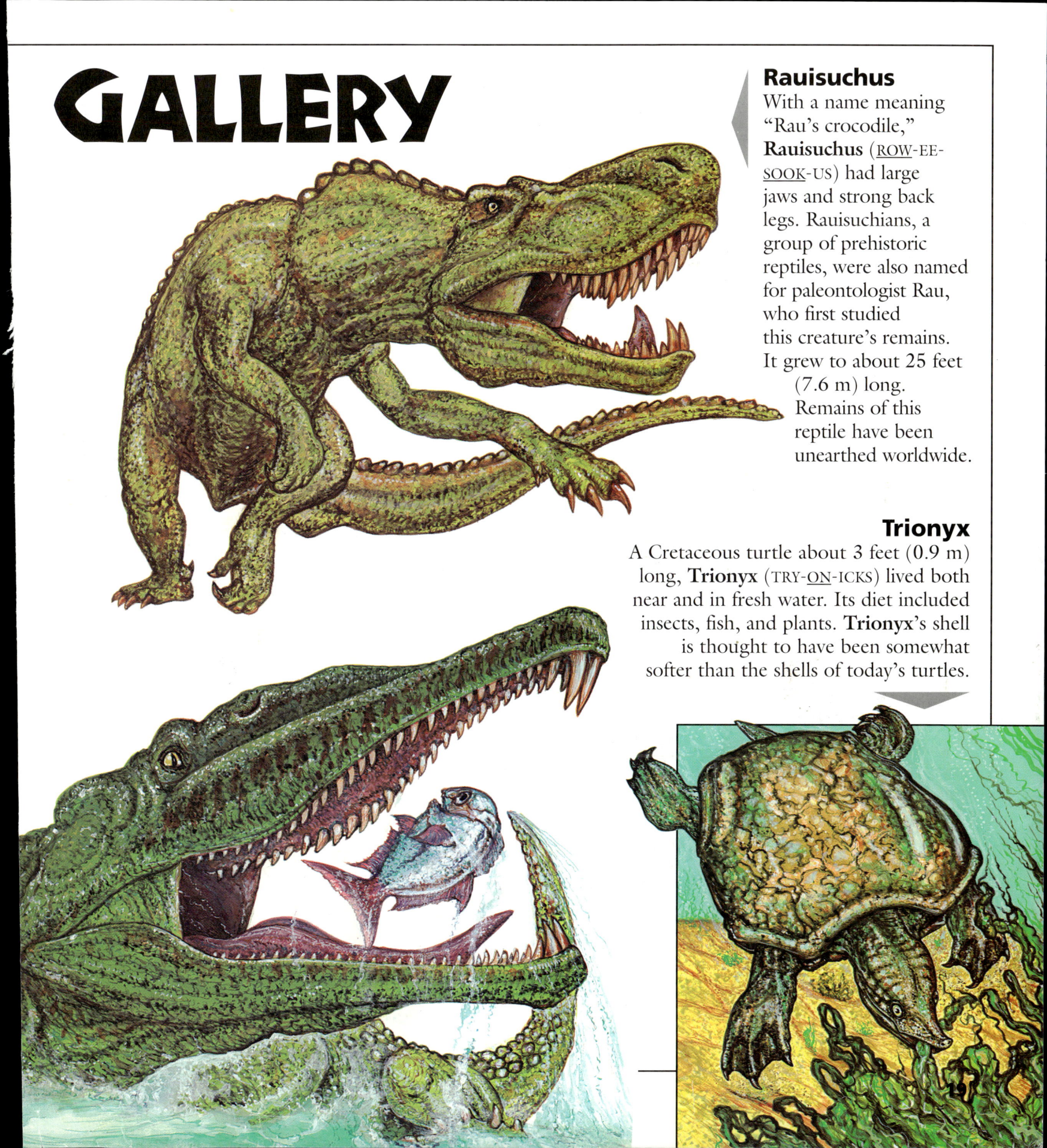

Rauisuchus
With a name meaning "Rau's crocodile," **Rauisuchus** (ROW-EE-SOOK-US) had large jaws and strong back legs. Rauisuchians, a group of prehistoric reptiles, were also named for paleontologist Rau, who first studied this creature's remains. It grew to about 25 feet (7.6 m) long. Remains of this reptile have been unearthed worldwide.

Trionyx
A Cretaceous turtle about 3 feet (0.9 m) long, **Trionyx** (TRY-ON-ICKS) lived both near and in fresh water. Its diet included insects, fish, and plants. **Trionyx**'s shell is thought to have been somewhat softer than the shells of today's turtles.

GALLERY

Cycads
During Jurassic times — the age of the giant sauropods — the large, fernlike leaves of palmlike **cycads** would have been a good source of food for herbivores. The sauropods were tall enough to reach the tops of the trees.

Seed-ferns
Small ferns were prolific during Jurassic times and must have provided thick ground cover. Even by Cretaceous times, grasses had not yet appeared.

Nilssonia
Nilssonia (NIL-SOHN-EE-AH) is an unusual large plant with distinctive leaves. Paleobotanists say it was widespread in Jurassic times.

OF PLANTS

Holly
During Cretaceous times, in regions of the world where the climate was temperate, a variety of shrubs as well as low-growing **holly** grew under the willow, sycamore, and poplar trees — trees that can still be found today. The holly leaves had prickles, so herbivorous dinosaurs probably preferred to munch on other more easily digestible plants in the forest undergrowth.

Magnolias
Until Cretaceous times, there were no flowering plants on planet Earth. Then, the first angiosperms appeared, including **magnolias**. They were pollinated by bees and possibly other insects, as well. According to some scientists, the **magnolias** of Cretaceous times were probably smaller than those found today.

LIVING FOSSILS

We are tempted to believe that, like the dinosaurs, every prehistoric species is dead and gone. Some creatures living today, however, had ancestors that lived during the age of the dinosaurs.

It had been a long day, but the fishermen were satisfied. The waters of the Indian Ocean that surrounded their native Comoros Islands, off the coast of southeastern Africa, teemed with fish. As usual, they would be putting into port at East London, South Africa, with their small boat groaning under the weight of their catch. As they emptied their nets on that December day in 1938, a peculiar specimen caught their eye. The slate-blue, 6-foot (1.8 m)-long creature thrashing for life was unlike any fish they had seen before. With its unusual snub nose and bulbous fins, it did not look at all appetizing. The fishermen wondered if the young lady scientist from the museum would be interested in their find.

When Marjorie Courtenay-Latimer set eyes on the strange fish, she was more than "interested." In fact, she could hardly contain her excitement. Lying in front of her was a creature that she had seen before only as a fossil, frozen in rock that was millions of years old. The shape of its body, fins, and tail matched those of a prehistoric **coelacanth**. This species was assumed to have become extinct, since no remains had ever been found that were less than 60 million years old. This did not seem to be the case after all.

Further finds

When another specimen was found fourteen years later, in 1952, it was examined by the Capetown fish expert Professor J. Smith, who pronounced that the **coelacanth** was, in fact, a living fossil, surviving unchanged for 400 million years.

How, then, had **coelacanths** survived, when their prehistoric companions had long since perished? This riddle puzzled scientists until 1987, when the German marine biologist Hans Fricke took a submersible craft down to explore the ocean bed around the Comoros Islands. There, in 550 feet (167 m) of water, he discovered a living **coelacanth** calmly exploring a crevice in some rocks on the seabed. Oddly enough, there did not seem to be very much marine life around it, although Fricke knew from remains of stomach contents found in **coelacanth** fossils that its ancestors dined on squid and other fish.

The key to the **coelacanth**'s survival, he claimed, was the reclusive life it led. He reasoned that the bulky **coelacanth** could not compete for food with more streamlined and, therefore, faster fish. Instead, it retreated to the depths of the water where the faster fish did not bother to go.

The discovery of other throwbacks

to prehistoric times, also found in remote parts of the world, seem to support his opinion. The tuatara lizard that lives on only a few remote islands off the coast of New Zealand, for example, is the only living survivor of the family of sphenolotid lizards that flourished in Late Triassic times. Scientists think the duck-billed platypus, an egg-laying mammal found only in Australia and dating back to Triassic times, is alive today because the continent broke away from the great prehistoric landmasses, thereby isolating its habitat.

IN THE SALTY SEAS

Dinosaurs may have ruled the land on Earth for 160 million years, but the oceans belonged to many species of frightening creatures.

Stegosaurus was much too busy quenching its thirst to notice that it had ventured into deep water. Suddenly, it spotted what it thought was another herbivore of its kind looking back at it from the watery depths. Of course, this was no more than its own reflection! The upright triangular shape slicing through the waves, however, was no such illusion. It was the fin of a razor-toothed shark, zeroing in for the kill.

The prehistoric seas were infested with sharks — just as tropical waters are today. In fact, they have barely changed in their 400 million years of existence.

Fossilized remains show that prehistoric sharks had streamlined bodies that could glide through the water at high speed, propelled by powerful fins and steered with magnificent fluked tails.

Their huge mouths had rows of sharp teeth, which were ideal for catching large numbers of fish and for tearing chunks of living flesh from fellow sea-dwellers. The sharks were equally adept at grabbing land creatures that strayed into the water, and they were able to drag even a hefty **Stegosaurus** to its watery doom.

Early oceans were also home to many other species — but not to dinosaurs. The farthest these monarchs of the land ever got in the sea was paddling up to their necks.

The most majestic of the sea-dwellers, however, were the plesiosaurs. Long-necked and bulky-bodied, they were the size of today's whales. Their relatives, the pliosaurs, such as 10-foot (3-m)-long **Peloneustes**, were smaller but made up for lack of size with ferocious natures. With mouths full of thin, pointed teeth, they would terrorize almost every other creature of the deep. Even the dolphinlike ichthyosaurs, which most sea creatures left alone, were not safe from huge pliosaurs, like **Kronosaurus**. This giant, short-necked marine reptile was named for the god Cronus, or Kronos, in Greek mythology. It lived in the southern prehistoric seas over what is now Australia and measured a frightening 56 feet (17 m) from nose to tail.

Ichthyosaurs were the most well-adapted of the prehistoric reptiles living in the seas. While others had to drag themselves onto exposed beaches to lay eggs — thereby leaving themselves open to attack from meat-eating dinosaurs on the lookout for an easy meal — ichthyosaurs gave birth to live young while still offshore. Fossils have shown embryos curled up inside their mothers' bodies. One unfortunate baby seems to have died at the same time as its mother, at the very moment of birth.

Despite being at home in the sea, however, ichthyosaurs died out long before most other sea reptiles, whose extinction is thought to have coincided with that of the dinosaurs.

WINGED LIZARDS

Although the dinosaurs had their feet firmly planted on the ground, some of their smaller reptilian cousins developed winglike flaps to glide from place to place.

The browsing sauropod was peacefully munching on lush leaves high up in the Jurassic trees. Suddenly, it was surprised by the sound of nearby rustling.

A strange-looking and frightened reptile had launched itself into midair — not realizing that it was safe, since the giant plant-eater ate no meat. Instead of dropping earthward like a stone, however, the **Draco** unfurled the winglike membranes attached to its sides and glided slowly and gracefully to a lower branch.

The prehistoric winged lizards could make short excursions through the air, but they could not actually fly. **Draco** could cover about 200 feet (61 m), but this was unusual. Most winged lizards could leap only about 50 feet (15 m). This was still a fair distance for creatures like Early Triassic **Coelosauravus**, only 16-18 inches (40-46 cm) long, to propel themselves as they glided between trees or from a lakeside take-off point to higher ground.

Expanding rib cages

Fossilized remains of winged lizards, such as Late Triassic **Icarosaurus** — named after the Greek architect and inventor who made wax wings in order to fly — show that they had four limbs, scaly skin, and a long tail. They also had elongated ribs protruding from the sides of their bodies. These ribs were covered by a thin membrane, which supported the creatures in flight, and could be — like those of **Daedalosaurus** — up to 13 inches (33 cm) across. Winged lizards spread out these flaps by expanding their rib cages.

Late Triassic **Kuehnosaurus**, meanwhile, had swept-back flaps, like a modern fighter plane. It could fold these flaps neatly against its body after landing, as could **Icarosaurus** and **Daedalosaurus**. This maneuver prevented the flaps from being caught as the creatures slithered through dense foliage.

The winged lizards used their unusual aerial skills to catch insects — which were either surprised and gobbled up as the lizards suddenly landed, or snatched from the air during flight. The lizards would also glide in an attempt to get themselves out of trouble if a predator approached. But many of the smaller, meat-eating dinosaurs, such as 10-foot (3-m)-long **Syntarsus**, would have made short work of a winged lizard. **Syntarsus** was probably swift enough on its feet to snap a lizard up before it could launch itself to safety.

Jungle survivor

For at least one species, the ability to glide allowed it to survive until the present day. In fact, prehistoric **Draco** still lives on in the jungles of Southeast Asia, where it is known as the **Flying Dragon**. Being only 10 inches (25 cm) long with a 4-inch (10-cm) wingspan, this mud-colored creature may also owe its survival to its ability to fade into the background, adapting over time to its changing surroundings.

READY FOR TAKE-OFF

The discovery of fossils in China that resemble dinosaurs with feathers could mean that these amazing prehistoric creatures are, in fact, still with us — but in the form of birds.

The small, furry **Megazostrodon** knew something was wrong as it raced along. A rustling of leaves had given away its potential attacker — a chicken-sized creature covered in downy spines. Sharp-sighted **Sinosauropteryx** had spotted its prey from a long way off, and was creeping in for the kill. A quick flex of its short, sinewy neck and the unfortunate **Megazostrodon** was clasped firmly in sharp-toothed jaws, ready to be swallowed by the hungry, birdlike reptile.

That **Sinosauropteryx** — meaning "first Chinese dragon feather" — was an early ancestor of birds is not in doubt, according to the scientists who examined fossils unearthed in Sihetun, northeastern China, in 1996. Like its modern counterparts, the 120-million-year-old creature had hollow bones, three-toed feet, and a birdlike neck. But most remarkable was its covering of fine filaments, each of which was up to 1.5 inches (3.8 cm) long. Experts claim these are the forerunners of feathers, which are necessary for flight.

Dinosaurlike

Sinosauropteryx also seems to have looked remarkably like such dinosaurs as **Velociraptor** and **Deinonychus**. Light-boned and fleet of foot, they shared the same bone structure as **Sinosauropteryx**, particularly in their arms, shoulders, and chest.

This momentous find mirrors a major discovery in Germany in 1861. The fossilized remains of **Archaeopteryx**, the first creature to be recognized as a bird, were found alongside those of **Compsognathus**, a chicken-sized, meat-eating dinosaur. The similarity of the skeletons was astonishing and led to the English nineteenth-century naturalist Sir Thomas Huxley's theory that birds were close relatives of the dinosaurs. Interestingly, though, the shoulder bones of

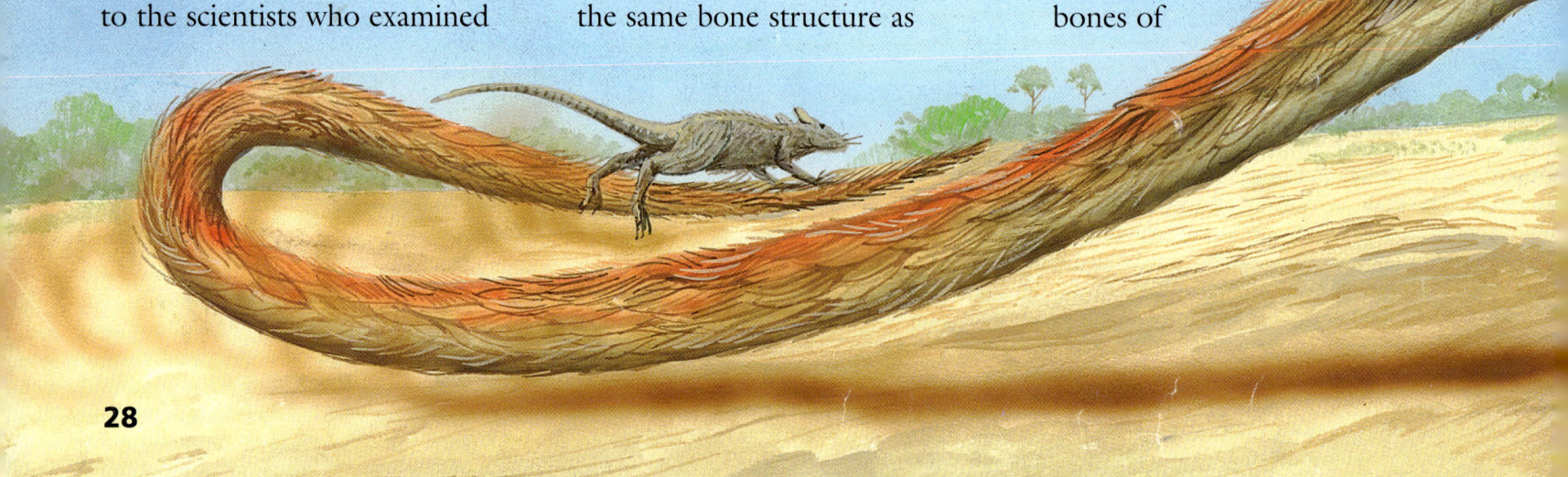

Archaeopteryx were not able to produce an effective up-and-down movement of its wings, so it probably did not fly too well.

Sinosauropteryx, like **Archaeopteryx**, had a mouth full of teeth. Experts who doubt that birds evolved from dinosaurs are quick to point out that this feature is not birdlike. Fossils found in the same place as **Sinosauropteryx** a few years earlier, however, showed two creatures, possibly a male and a smaller female, with curved, toothless, horny beaks.

Named **Confuciusornis sancta**, after the Chinese philosopher Confucius, these remains were as old as **Archaeopteryx** and also had feathers.

The link between dinosaurs and birds certainly seems very strong, to judge by fossil evidence.

GLOSSARY

adapting — changing to be suitable for different conditions or for a different purpose.

amber — a somewhat clear, brownish-yellow material that is the hardened resin of prehistoric pine trees.

ammonites — extinct, soft-bodied aquatic creatures that had tentacles and hard, coiled shells.

belemnites — prehistoric marine animals that resembled squids.

buoyant — able to float on or rise to the surface of water.

carnivorous — relating to a meat-eating animal.

chondrosteans — prehistoric fish with bony armor around the head and oversized tail fins.

coprolites — fossilized dung, or animal droppings.

Cretaceous times — the final era of the dinosaurs, lasting from 144-65 million years ago.

disperse — to scatter or spread widely.

embryo — an animal in the first stage of development before birth.

evolved — adapted and changed over a period of time to suit changing environments.

flukes — the flattened parts of the tail of a marine animal, such as those of whales.

foliage — the leaves of a tree, shrub, or plant.

fronds — the leaves of a fern or palm tree.

herbivorous — relating to a plant-eating animal.

horsetail — a type of flowerless plant that is related to ferns.

ichthyosaurs — extinct marine reptiles that had fishlike bodies and long snouts.

Jurassic times — the middle era of the dinosaurs, lasting from 213-144 million years ago.

marauding — roaming and looting, as in a raid.

marsupial — an animal that carries its newborn young in a pouch on the mother's abdomen.

paleobotanists — scientists who study the fossilized remains of plants.

phytosaur — a member of a group of Late Triassic reptiles similar to crocodiles.

pliosaurs — large prehistoric marine reptiles that had huge jaws and spiked teeth.

proboscis — a long, flexible snout.

prolific — producing young or fruit in great numbers; very productive.

pterosaurs — extinct flying reptiles.

rauisuchian — a crocodilelike reptile from Late Triassic times.

remains — a dead body; something left over.

reptiles — cold-blooded, mostly egg-laying animals, such as lizards, turtles, and many prehistoric creatures.

sauropod — any member of a group of long-necked, plant-eating dinosaurs, mainly from Jurassic times, which had small heads and five-toed feet.

symbiosis — the relationship of two or more different kinds of organisms that live in close association in a way that is beneficial to both or all.

temperate — neither very hot or very cold; avoiding extremes.

trawl — to catch fish by dragging an open jaw or net along the bottom of a body of water.

Triassic times — the first era of the dinosaurs, lasting from 249-213 million years ago.

More Books to Read

Creatures of Long Ago: Dinosaurs. Jane Buxton, Editor (National Geographic Society)

Dinosaurs: Monster Reptiles of a Bygone Era. Secrets of the Animal World (series). Eulalia García (Gareth Stevens)

Dinosaurs and How They Lived. Steve Parker (Dorling Kindersley)

Dinosaurs and Other Prehistoric Animals. Maria Flügel (Gareth Stevens)

Explore the World of Prehistoric Life. Dougal Dixon (Western Publishing)

Living Dinosaurs. Jeff Davidson (Willowisp Press)

Living Fossils: Animals That Have Withstood the Test of Time. James Martin (Crown Publishers)

Mighty Mammals of the Past. John Stidworthy (Silver Burdett)

The New Dinosaur Collection (series). (Gareth Stevens)

Prehistoric Marine Reptiles. Judy A. Massare (Franklin Watts)

Pteranodon. Ron Wilson (Rourke Enterprises)

World of Dinosaurs (series). (Gareth Stevens)

Videos

Did Comets Kill the Dinosaurs? (Gareth Stevens)

Dinosaurs and Other Prehistoric Animals. (Seesaw Video)

Dinosaurs and Strange Creatures. (Concord Video)

Dinosaurs: The Terrible Lizards. (AIMS Media)

Learning About Dinosaurs. (Trans-Atlantic Video)

Nova: The Case of the Flying Dinosaur. (Live Home Video)

Web Sites

www.clpgh.org/cmnh/discovery/

www.dinodon.com/index.html

www.dinofest.org/

www.dinosauria.com/

www.dinosociety.org/

www.ZoomDinosaurs.com

Due to the dynamic nature of the Internet, some web sites stay current longer than others. To find additional web sites, use a reliable search engine with one or more of the following keywords to help you locate more information about dinosaurs. Keywords: *coelacanth, dinosaurs, fossils, paleontology, prehistoric, pterosaurs.*

INDEX

Alphadon 17
amber 11
ammonites 6
amphibians 9, 18
Archaeopteryx 28, 29

belemnites 6
birds 5, 28, 29

carnivores 5, 10, 17, 18
Caturus 7
chondrosteans 7
coelacanth 22
Coelophysis 10
Coelosauravus 26
Comoros Islands 22
Compsognathus 28
Confuciusornis sancta 29
coprolites 13
Cornuboniscus 7
Cretaceous era 5, 6, 7, 8, 9, 12, 13, 18, 19, 20, 21
cycads 20

Daedalosaurus 27
Deinonychus 28
Dimorphodon 14
Draco 26, 27
duck-billed platypus 23

Earth 6, 10, 12, 21, 24
evolution 7, 9, 13, 14, 29
extinction 6, 22, 25

fish 6, 7, 9, 14, 18, 19, 22
flowering plants 12, 13
Flying Dragon 27
fossils 6, 7, 11, 13, 14, 18, 22-23, 25, 27, 28, 29

Gonipholis 9

habitats 8-9, 23
herbivores 13, 14, 20, 21, 24, 26
holly 21

Icarosaurus 27
ichthyosaurs 25
insects 5, 9, 10, 11, 12, 13, 19, 21, 27

Jurassic era 6, 7, 8, 14, 16, 20, 26
Jurassic Park 11

Kronosaurus 25
Kuehnosaurus 27

Labyrinthodont 18
Longisquama 14

magnolias 12, 13, 21
mammals 5, 16, 17, 23
marsupials 17
Megazostrodon 17, 28
Metoposaurus 9

Nilssonia 20

Ouranosaurus 8, 9

Parasaurolophus 13
Peloneustes 25
phytosaurs 18
plesiosaurs 25
pliosaurs 25
Podopteryx 14
pollination 12, 13, 21
predators 6, 9, 10, 14, 16, 27
prey 5, 9, 28
Proganochelys 9
Pteranodon 14
Pterodactylus 14
pterosaurs 5, 14

rauisuchians 18, 19
Rauisuchus 19
remains 7, 14, 16, 18, 19, 22, 25, 27, 28, 29
reptiles 5, 9, 10, 14-15, 16, 18, 19, 25, 26, 28
Rhamphorhynchus 14
Ricinulei 11
Rutiodon 9, 18

Sarchosuchus 8, 9
sauropods 6, 14, 20, 26
Saurosuchus 18
seed-ferns 9, 20
sharks 24
Sinosauropteryx 28, 29
sphenolotid lizards 23
Stegosaurus 24, 25
symbiosis 13
Syntarsus 27

therapsid 16
Triassic era 6, 8, 9, 10, 14, 16, 17, 18, 23, 26, 27
Triconodon 16
Trionyx 9, 19
Tritylodont 16
tuatara lizards 23

Velociraptor 28

winged lizards 26, 27

Xiphacinus 7